Praise for *The Bi*
Secret of Cry

"As a therapist, an expert on fear and self-esteem, and a mom who adopted, I see this book as an absolutely necessary read. This story teaches kids to recognize, accept, and thrive in their uniqueness rather than fear it. It normalizes their experience and empowers them."

—Nancy Stella, PhD, PsyD
Author of *Fear Traps: Escape the Triggers that Keep You Stuck*

"I like that the Birdfish actually ended up forgiving the ones who were bullying her and became friends with them. I also like how being different ended up being a good thing that helped others."

—Camille
10 years old, Tennessee

"*The Birdfish and the Secret of Crystal Island* is an endearing story that addresses well both the challenges and beauty of an intercultural life. I was struck by how much this quirky story helped me reflect on pieces of my own journey, having personally grown up torn between two cultures, never fully finding a place in one nor the other.

It accurately showcases the struggles and pain of trying to find your place when it seems like there is nowhere you fit. At the same time, it highlights the profound value in being different. The story gives the reader hope for that same value to be true of themselves.

Being an educator who works with intercultural students, I believe The Birdfish and the Secret of Crystal Island will help kids identify their own challenges and find value in their uniqueness."

—Rebekah Sharp
International Educator

"This story had amazing characters. It had a vivid setting that I enjoyed trying to imagine in my head.

I think that Staraku's journey was kind of like my own life. I live in a different place that is far from where I was raised, so it's also hard for me to make friends because they speak a different language where I live now.

I think this is a very good book for kids my age to read, especially if they have migrated to a different country. I think a lot of people my age can sympathize with the emotions that Staraku is going through. And if they can't, it will be interesting for them to learn how others feel."

—Isaiah
12 years old, California to Indonesia

"I loved this book! I could picture all the characters. It was almost like a movie, the story was so real. I learned something while Staruku was learning too. It was good to see the other characters figuring out how to work together."

"I like this book because it showed that the Birdfish didn't need to be like everybody else to belong. The story was really fun to read."

"Young readers will be delighted by this story of Staraku, a courageous, small Birdfish who runs away from her problems only to meet friends who help her discover her power to face them. This book will be a helpful resource for adults as they help children navigate our changing society. It cleverly addresses themes of identity, bullying, friendship, and forgiveness. As a storyteller and author, I was captivated. As a former children's literature instructor, I will be recommending this to teachers!"

"Being adopted from Nepal, I've spent a lot of my life feeling different. This is the book I needed when I was younger."

THE BIRDFISH
AND THE SECRET OF
CRYSTAL ISLAND

KATSURA SUZUKI
ILLUSTRATED BY DEE DELOY

The Birdfish and the Secret of Crystal Island
Copyright © 2021 Katsura Suzuki

First paperback edition November 2021

Cover painting by Dee DeLoy, Newstart Art
nickdanger@newstartart.com
Published by Berry Powell Press
Glendora, California
www.berrypowellpress.com

ISBN: 978-1-7363953-4-9 (paperback)
ISBN: 978-1-7363953-5-6 (ebook)
Library of Congress Control Number: 2021921100

www.drkatsurasuzuki.com

I would like to dedicate this book to my son, Michel, and my daughter, Chanelle. They inspired me to write this book.

CONTENTS

NOTE TO PARENTS

The story of the Birdfish is incredibly personal to me. In fact, it is *my* story. And perhaps it is yours or your child's too.

Let me tell you a little about me. I am an only child, born and raised in Japan. Growing up, everyone knew me as "the tea ceremony master's daughter," and assumed I would follow in my mother's footsteps to become a master myself. So, at the age of five, I started my training. I sat still and quiet for hours at a time learning the ritual of making and serving tea. While I was supposed to be meditating, I actually spent most of those hours wishing I were anywhere else. I never quite fit the mold.

As soon as I could, I left Japan on a mission to find my own purpose. I moved to the US and eventually Switzerland, where I started my family and spent the next thirty-five years in Swiss-based financial advisory services. My work, my family, my life—it was all a blend of East and West. But in both places, I never fully felt like I belonged.

It wasn't until I hit a crisis that I started having these vivid dreams. In them was a half-bird, half-fish creature with a funny little mentor who helped her find her power. I would wake up and start writing. Those dreams became the basis for this book.

The dreams also prompted me to start meditating again—this time for myself, not to please my parents. In meditation, I remembered the lost lessons of my childhood. Having cast them aside long ago, I asked them to guide me again.

It was only then, when I began to embrace both parts of me, that I began to feel whole.

It's hard growing up in a world made of so many different types of people. At some point we all ask, "Who am I?" and "Where do I fit in?" I suspect there is a little Birdfish in all of us.

My greatest wish is that your children—your silly, quirky, complex, beautiful, mold-breaking kids—will find their freedom and purpose in being exactly who they are. I hope this book will help them realize that what makes them different is what gives them a unique purpose. Along with the Birdfish, we can all discover our own power and help make the world a more welcoming place.

Warmly,

Dr. Katsura Suzuki

Learn more about Dr. Suzuki at www.drkatsurasuzuki.com.

CHAPTER 1

"I love this place," Staraku sighed as she glided on the surface of the glassy blue ocean. She headed toward the large rock formation that rose from the sea. For obvious reasons, it was called The Rock. It protected the east side of the island from the wild ocean.

The warm breeze caught her outstretched wings and moved her effortlessly through the smooth water. She tried to relax, allowing the bright yellow sun to warm her scales. A slight ripple in the sea rocked her back and forth. All was calm.

Staraku's webbed toes bumped into the rocks just under the water. The rocks were covered with a seaweed forest. Their glossy leaves tickled her scales as they reached toward the sun. "I'm all alone," she assured herself, looking down at her own reflection. She reached her wing to the water and touched the mirror image. The Birdfish on the other side rippled.

Staraku studied her reflection for a moment. Her feathery wings were as full and strong as any other bird's, and they could take her anywhere through the air. Her colorful scales were as vibrant and slick as any other fish's, and they allowed her to dash through the water with ease. She could be a great bird, or a great fish. But why did she have to be both at the same time? She never knew.

She and her reflection frowned at each other.

"What am I really? I'm a bird, but I'm also a fish. I'm a fish, but I'm also a bird." Admitting what was in her heart, she said to no one in particular, "I don't really know who I am or where I belong." She stirred a wing in the water and her reflection disappeared beneath the froth.

I DON'T REALLY KNOW WHO I AM OR WHERE I BELONG.

Looking up at the empty horizon gave her mixed feelings too. Part of her wanted to see a flock of birds above her or a school of fish swimming by so she could join them and be surrounded by friends on all sides. But in reality, the birds and the fish wanted nothing to do with her. They weren't her friends, never had been, and most likely never would be. They made it very clear they didn't want her on their island.

She watched herself nodding in agreement as her reflection became still and clear again. Hiding behind The Rock, exploring the place between the sky and the sea, was the only time she had ever felt that she fit in.

"OUCH!" Staraku leapt out of the water as something sharp clipped her toe from beneath the surface. Something thrashed in the water below, and bubbles rose to the surface. "What was that?" She thrust her head under the water.

Her face was quickly surrounded by clusters of small blue, green, and brown fish. Their tiny teeth bit her fiercely. "Oh, no," she said, her face dropping. "Not you again!"

She cried out as the tiny bites stung her feet and belly. She heard the fish calling out through the water, "Get out of here!" and "Fly away, beach rat!"

Before she had time to pull her head out of the sea, three little fish were already latched onto her fins and wings. She threw herself forward and backward, hoping to fling them off, but they were able to hold fast. The water foamed around her as more fish arrived to torment her. How fast they darted! They moved all together all at once. Staraku thought that might slow them down, but it only made them swifter.

"How did you find me here?" The desperate question slipped out between her shrieks. Staraku swatted the three on her tail with a wing, finally knocking them off. Then she rapidly flipped her webbed feet back and forth in the water and flapped her wings to escape. She gained a little speed. But just before she could rise into the sky, one foul-mouthed fish popped his head above the water. He shouted, "Get out of our ocean!"

Against her better judgment, she turned back to look. Of course, it was Buntu. Everyone followed him. In fact, he probably led them here, though he didn't used to be so popular. In fact, other fish used to tease *him* mercilessly.

He was bigger than the others, about the same size as Staraku. Plus, his scales were the same color. Seeing this similarity, the other fish used to swarm around him asking, "Why do you look alike? Are you cousins? Where are *your* feathers, big guy?" He said he'd rather be cooked for dinner than have anything to do with "that freak." To defend his own reputation, he became the leader of those out to get her.

Now, making her humiliation worse, Buntu shouted one last cruelty. "You thought you could hide from us? This is our island, and you don't belong here! Now get out!"

Staraku heard the wild laughter of the fish. Their heads peeked out of their ocean to see her reaction. Her cheeks grew hot.

Staraku frantically broke into the sky. She quickly gained height to escape the fish in the water below. She let out a big sigh. *Why do they hate me so much?* She might have started to cry, except she noticed slick shadows passing over her head. She knew at once what that meant. The birds had also found and followed her.

Staraku looked at the sky and then back down at the sea. *I'm trapped!* She panted in panic. Before she knew it, dozens of birds whipped past her, spinning her out of control with their thick, feathery shoulders.

"Hey gills!" They laughed at her. She toppled through the air like a palm frond in a storm. While she was still dizzy, the biggest bird, Tori, snatched Staraku's neck in her beak.

"Hey, let go!" the Birdfish cried.

Tori flew down toward the water at a dangerous speed. "I'm just trying to help *you* get back to the ocean where *you* belong!" she said.

Staraku thought she might be dragged under the water where those nasty fish were. Right at the surface of the water, Tori pulled back and dangled Staraku upside down. Staraku's head was so close to the water that it splashed against her face. She wriggled away and righted herself as the birds dove in for their second attack.

Salty tears pooled in her eyes as she pumped her wings as hard as she possibly could. She heard the thrashing of fish in the water beneath her and the angry squawks of the birds above. "Go home, guppy! You don't belong in the air with us birds," Tori shouted. The insult trailed behind her, staying around long after she'd gotten away.

She flew swiftly along the surface of the water. The birds landed together on The Rock.

Staraku heard laughter as she sped away. "We sure showed her!"

CHAPTER 2

To be certain she was free, Staraku flew to the highest mountains on the island. The mountains rose straight out of the sea on the far side of the island. There was no way for the fish to get there, and none of the birds liked to fly up that high. It was just too much of an effort.

Once over the mountains, she flew down into a deep valley at the island's center. Down she soared, circling deeper and deeper. Bursting through the canopy of tall trees and vines, she landed on soft soil.

Under the thick umbrella of trees, beams of orange light poked through. Streams trickled around her, but they were too shallow for swimming. The sky rustled with branches, making it too crowded for flying. Plopping down on the forest floor. The exhaustion of the day fell over her like a heavy blanket.

I don't get it. I look like both of them! But then again, I don't look like either of them. Anger pulsed through her. *Why is that such a problem? Is being different so horrible?* She had no answers to her questions. It had always been that way.

"Yet again," she said aloud, although she knew no one could hear her, "They're not very nice to each other either!" It was true. It was a big island—the birds and fish *could* have chosen to live on opposite sides to keep the peace. But both groups wanted to live at the beach on the eastern shore.

Since the island was in the middle of the ocean, the waves battered against it on all sides. It was dangerous for smaller fish to swim close to the island. They could be smashed against the rocks and sand. Even the larger fish had to be careful if a storm arose.

But on the eastern side of the island was a small lagoon. The little pool of water was protected by land on all sides. There was one way in and one way out, like a little door. It was so narrow, bigger fish couldn't even get through. Smaller fish laid their eggs there. The babies were safe and sound until they hatched and grew large enough to join their parents in the open sea.

Surrounding the lagoon grew a grove of trees—a tall forest with deep roots. The trees were so strong that they stood firm even in the most terrible storms. They were perfect for the birds to build their nests, lay their eggs, and raise their families.

While both birds and fish wanted to live at the lagoon, they didn't want to live there *together*. Even though the birds lived in the trees and the fish lived in the water, their two worlds were right next to each other. They were not interested in sharing.

Staraku looked around as she thought all this through. *They are quite self-centered. Not only that, they speak completely different languages.* Staraku understood both languages, and always knew what they were saying. But the birds didn't understand fish-language and the fish didn't understand bird-language. So, they really had no idea what the other was saying.

This didn't stop them from screaming insults at each other. The birds swooped in low and dangled their feet in the water causing ripples which upset the eggs below. "Take your eggs someplace else! This is our beach!" they said.

The fish popped their heads out of the ocean and spewed water at the birds—trying to soak their wings so they couldn't fly. "This is our lagoon! We're not going anywhere! You're the ones who don't belong here!"

The fight over the lagoon raged on with no solution in sight. Staraku didn't know how it would ever end. *Even if they did speak the same language, I doubt that it would help. They simply won't try to listen.* Staraku realized something. *The birds and fish only want to win. That means everyone else has to lose.*

> EVEN IF THEY DID SPEAK THE SAME LANGUAGE, I DOUBT THAT IT WOULD HELP. THEY SIMPLY WON'T TRY TO LISTEN.

Yet, with all this conflict, there was one thing that both the birds and the fish agreed on: they both hated Staraku. They both believed there was no place on this island for a Birdfish. So here she was, in hiding, deep in the forest under the long, feathery fern leaves.

She looked around at the trees that surrounded her, as if they were standing guard. She always felt safe in the forest. *I wish the trees could talk,* she thought to herself. *I'd have all of the friends I would ever need. What a crazy thought,* she scolded herself.

Sitting alone in the dark, Staraku thought hard. *How can I fit in with the birds or the fish?* Because Staraku always had to take care of herself, she'd become very independent. When she wanted something, she'd figure out how to get it.

Looking around, she noticed the big fern leaves lying on the ground like feathers. She decided they'd make a nice place to sleep. She got up to make a bed for herself, but she accidentally stepped on a leaf. Sticky white sap from the rubber tree nearby got all over her foot, and now everything was sticking to her. *Oh, no! How will I get that off of me?*

She took a small rock and started scraping off the sap from her foot. *This stuff is very, very sticky!* Then a perfect solution came to her. *Wait, that's it!* "I've got it," she whispered to the night.

By beams of moonlight, Staraku squeezed out the white, sticky sap that flowed in the branches of the rubber tree. Then she gathered long feathery leaves from the giant ferns that filled the inner forest floor. Carefully, she spread the white sap over the leaves until they looked splotchy like milk. The color was slightly lighter than her sandy-gold feathers. *They'll blend just fine.*

She twisted her neck down to secure each leaf to her body. One by one, into the night, she secured the ferns in the exact pattern of bird feathers. If her plan succeeded, she would completely cover her scales with leaves—she'd look just like the birds. The perfect disguise! *And then I'll finally fit in.* She assured herself the plan would work, and then drifted off to sleep with a hopeful smile on her face.

CHAPTER 3

I n the morning, Staraku made her way from the tropical forest out to the water's edge where she looked down on her rippling reflection to see how she looked. "Perfect," she chirped, giving herself a high-five. Sighing, she silently wished she could always look this way—simple, just a bird. Cutting through the early morning fog, she flew toward The Rock. She knew she'd certainly find birds there.

Staraku was grateful the ferns on her body stayed on as she flew. Soon she saw The Rock in the distance. Something about it felt a bit daring—to be surrounded by the ocean on all sides. Sometimes there would be plenty of craggy surfaces to perch on. Other times, it was almost entirely swallowed by the sea as the waves threatened to eat it whole. You never knew what you'd find. For a bird, it was clearly the place to be.

She landed smoothly and spied a small group of birds chatting nearby. Trying not to draw attention to herself, she casually walked around looking this way and that, as if she was completely unaware of the collection of birds chatting away. Finally, she waddled up near them. They gave her a funny look, but they didn't immediately attack her. *So far, so good.* Things were going well, thanks to her new disguise.

A few of them bobbed their heads in greeting and then continued with their conversation. They chattered about the sand crabs. They all loved catching those tasty little creatures. Staraku preferred eating the fruit of the island or the yummy plants under the sea, but she chimed in when appropriate.

"They taste different this season, eh?" one asked.

"Last year's catch was better," another said.

"Last year's catch was puny!" another shot back.

Some other birds joined them, and no one took notice of Staraku. It was delightful. She relished in the simplicity of blending in. *Things are always so complicated when you don't fit in. It's so much easier when you look like everyone else.*

"Make way!" a bird called from overhead. The birds all knew what that meant. They stepped back and made a circle for Tori and her entourage. There was loud swoosh of wings, and Tori landed in the center of the circle. Then *plop, plop, plop* came her three loyal protectors. Tori flung her head to the side, flashing her shiny dark blue feathers at everyone.

All of the birds knew that Tori was a bully of a bird and crossing her was a bad idea. The circle of birds stood very still, trying to look like they all adored her. Tori strutted around, eying her fans and trying to catch anyone who might not be loyal. Staraku squatted down behind a group of taller birds, trying to be as still and invisible as possible. Tori seemed satisfied with the flock.

One of her henchmen said, "Tori is going to make an announcement!"

Tori stepped up on one of the rocks, so that everyone could see her. She opened her beak, but before she could speak, an ocean wave slapped the rockface behind her. The icy water sprayed directly on Tori's head. She was drenched. She gasped and caught her breath. A few of them laughed nervously but promptly went silent when they saw the rage in Tori's eyes.

"Did I hear someone laughing?" Tori shrieked. Silence. All eyes were on Tori, which was unfortunate because none of the birds—not even Staraku—noticed what was coming. Off in the distance, a huge wave was taking form. It looked like a small whale was swimming just under the surface, lifting the water up over its back. Growing quickly in size and speed, a huge wall of water headed straight for The Rock.

One bird happened to look up at the last moment. "Um, guys—"

It was too late. The wave arched over the rock, suspended in air, and then crashed down. It leveled everything and everyone on it. Caught off guard like the others, Staraku felt the punch of the wave smash her into the stony surface of The Rock. It scraped her across the jagged stone. The water's force threw the other birds on top of her. They clung to each other to keep from being washed into the choppy sea. Tori, who was on the highest and most vulnerable point, was swept off the edge with a loud splash.

"Help! Save me!" cried Tori, flailing in the water. "I can't swim!"

"Oh no," yelled a bird next to Staraku. "That's Tori!"

Another bird called out, "Someone save her!"

"Who can do that?" asked another in the crowd. "None of us can swim either!"

Staraku stared down at the struggling bird for a moment. *She's getting what she deserves.* Staraku felt guilty for her thoughts. Tori had always been especially cruel to her, scoffing at her scales and calling her Fish Face. Staraku didn't really *want* to save her.

The birds flew down closer to the water trying to help. "Grab onto my feet!" yelled one of her guards. Tori reached up, but another wave came and whisked her further out to sea. Staraku knew none of the other birds could go into the swirling water. The waves would swallow them whole.

"I don't see her anymore!" someone gasped.

She'll drown if I don't get her. I'm the only one who can do it. With that thought, Staraku dove headfirst into the churning ocean. At first, the water was too cloudy to see through it. But as the bubbles cleared, she saw Tori sinking beneath her. Grabbing her by her tail feathers, Staraku dragged her heavy body up to the surface.

It took all of Staraku's strength to drag Tori up the side of The Rock. She was already a pretty big bird. Now heavy with water, it was sheer determination that gave Staraku the power to get her out of the sea. Tori was water-logged and coughing. One rocky ledge at a time, Staraku pulled her back to the top of the wet rock.

SHE'LL DROWN IF I DON'T GET HER.
I'M THE ONLY ONE WHO CAN DO IT.

Tori looked quite pathetic. Her beautiful feathers stuck awkwardly in all directions around her face and body. She hacked loudly, water spilling from her beak.

The birds quickly ran past Staraku to help Tori get back up on her feet. "Are you okay?" one asked.

"Step back, everyone. Give her air!" a worried bird said.

"Where is the bird who saved her?" another asked.

The flock looked around and when they saw Staraku, everyone stopped and stared. Tori wiped the water from her eyes and could now see clearly. In front of her was Staraku, with drippy wings and shimmering scales of aquamarine.

"What?" Tori shook her head and squinted, trying to understand what creature had just rescued her.

"It's the Birdfish!" someone hollered. Staraku looked down at herself and then covered her body with her wings. Her leafy disguise had been torn off by her plunge into the sea. All that remained were the sticky white patches of rubber tree sap that once held her fake feathers.

"The Birdfish saved Tori," another bird whispered.

Tori stood up on wobbly legs. For a moment, Staraku saw a flicker of gratitude in the bird's eyes. She thought Tori might actually thank her. But before Tori could open her mouth, one of the birds screamed, "She's a fraud!" Immediately, the other birds joined in with more accusations.

"She tried to fool us into believing she was a bird!"

"Imposter!"

Staraku looked at Tori with desperate eyes, hoping she'd stand up for her, but for once, Tori remained silent. Though Staraku had just pulled her from the wave's terrible grip, Tori offered nothing in her defense.

With a burst of flapping wings and voices blaring, more birds arrived on The Rock. Their expressions went from confusion to realization, from horror to anger. Pushing in closer, it was clear to Staraku that the swarm of birds was about to attack.

Staraku took off like a bullet, straight up in the air, hoping to get ahead of the others. She beat her wings as fiercely as she could. Then she flipped over and aimed directly toward the water, where she knew the birds couldn't follow her. She scolded herself. *I should have let her drown. I was such a fool to think anyone on this island would ever be my friend!*

As she shot into the water, the ocean absorbed her salty tears. The waves washed off all the milky glue from her scales. The sunlight danced through the waves, shimmering against her scales to comfort her.

I've got to get out of here before the fish show up. She swam swiftly through the water catching a current that sped her far into open waters. Once she knew she was out of reach from anyone on her island, Staraku came back to the surface. Floating on the surface, she cried out, "Why was I made this way?" But no one heard her, so no one answered.

WHY WAS I MADE THIS WAY?

Her sadness was replaced by a jolt of anger pulsing through her body. And then she made a life-changing decision.

Staraku flapped her wings and lifted off into the air. Heading away from her island home, she declared to herself, "No matter how long it takes me or how far I have to go, I'm going to find someone who will be my friend."

CHAPTER 4

S taraku had no idea where she was heading. When she got tired of flying, she swam. When she got tired of swimming, she flew. Between the soft, rolling waves and the shimmering sunlight, the morning's horror washed away.

The sun moved overhead and beat down on her with its heat. From time to time, she flew over a number of islands—some large and some tiny. "Not far enough away," she decided.

A low-lying island came up on the horizon. As she neared its shore, she saw that it was dry and windy, and covered in swirling orange sand. It was flat, void of mountains or even hills. It didn't look like anything could grow there. *What an awful place to live. No trees to build a nest in and no streams or rivers to swim and sleep in. I'll keep going.*

The next island was lush and green. *Could this be a good place to land?* As Staraku flew down to see who lived there, she noticed that the closer she got, the louder the buzz of voices became—the screeching of monkeys, the loud cawing of birds, and massive fish with jagged teeth splashing in and out of the water.

No way! She shook her head and made a sharp turn off to the right. *I can't let them see me.* Just the thought of finding more creatures who would hate her made her feel jittery with nerves. She flew on.

But as the sky turned a burnt orange, she knew the sun had run out of patience for her. It was now setting. Her wings ached and her stomach grumbled. The heat simmered around her. Her throat was raspy with thirst.

I have to find someplace before dark. The wind whipped up as night began to fall. *Oh, where do I go?*

And then, just as she thought she might have to turn back to an island she had passed, a glimmer way off in the distance caught her eye, "What is that?" she wondered out loud, "Certainly not an island. Islands don't shine."

But the closer she flew, the brighter the island glowed. Staraku flapped her wings faster. *What's making this place shimmer with light?* As she neared it, her eyes widened. She saw that the island was covered in millions of crystals of all sizes. Some were as large as boulders, and others were tiny little pebbles. They caught the setting sunlight and tossed it back into the air. She'd never seen anything like it.

SHE SAW THAT THE ISLAND WAS COVERED IN MILLIONS OF CRYSTALS OF ALL SIZES. SOME WERE AS LARGE AS BOULDERS, AND OTHERS WERE TINY LITTLE PEBBLES. THEY CAUGHT THE SETTING SUNLIGHT AND TOSSED IT BACK INTO THE AIR. SHE'D NEVER SEEN ANYTHING LIKE IT.

The scales on her body shined as the light reflected on her golds, greens, and blues. Right in the center of the island stood a tall mountain, gloriously covered in crystals. Streams of shimmering water flowed down the sides of its brilliant slopes. The water cut tracks down to the crystal-covered beaches. She smiled. *Ah, streams to swim in.*

Staraku flew further down to explore. Along the streams were groves of tall trees. They had thick, wrinkled trunks and lanky vines that swooped to the island floor. Crystals clung to each branch like fallen stars from the sky. Her wings beat softer as she took it all in.

Are there any mean creatures hiding in the forest? To get a better look, Staraku glided down to inspect. There were no fish in the streams. No birds in the trees. "I think this could be a very good place to spend the night," she said aloud as she landed on the crystal-encrusted sand.

Staraku paused, tilting her head slightly for any sounds of creatures below. She heard nothing but the bubbling of the water across the stones and the tinkling of crystals in the breeze. "It's safe here," she reassured herself.

So exhausted from her ordeal and frantic escape, Staraku didn't even try to make a nest for herself. Nor did she want to venture into the ocean to sleep. She feared there might be a school of fish hiding beneath the waters. The Birdfish walked up the beach and settled in at the base of a large tree. She used her beak to knock the sand off her scales. She fluffed her feathers and snuggled into a little nook just the right size for her to rest in. The sun set and the crystals' glow dimmed. Staraku barely closed her eyes before she fell into a deep sleep.

* * *

When she woke, the sun was bright. It was nearly noon, she guessed. She could barely see, with all of the crystals reflecting the sun back into her eyes.

"How did I sleep so long?" she asked out loud, watching and listening to the waves crashing to the shore.

"You must have been very tired," a deep voice rang out from deep in the forest.

Staraku jumped to her feet, smoothing her feathers quickly, trying to look bigger than she was.

"Who said that?" Fear filled her heart. She puffed her chest out, preparing for someone big and fierce to appear. She strained her eyes into the shadows, but it was too dark to see anyone.

Beside the tree was a fuzzy green mound dotted with crystals and tall grasses atop. The green and yellow fronds shifted as something—no, some*one*—moved through them. Staraku couldn't see what the creature was, but from the sound of its footsteps, she guessed it was something horrible and hideously scary.

"Another bully," she whispered with bitterness. She thought about flying, but she didn't know if the monster could fly. *What chance do I have of escaping?*

As the grasses parted further, Staraku saw a glowing light. Perhaps it was the ruler of this island. *Maybe I can talk my way out of this.* "I am so sorry to intrude upon your island, Your Majesty," she babbled. "I can leave right away if you don't want me here. You know, no one really wants me around, so I won't be offended if you want me to go . . ."

The grasses parted further as she pressed her back against the tree. She closed her eyes, afraid to even look at what enemy she was about to face.

CHAPTER 5

Staraku heard a small cough. Squinting one eye open, she saw a very small creature step out from between the trees—a little blue being with a round head and soft eyes. He wore a pair of thin spectacles. And he glowed as if there was a little star inside of him. The light shone around and through him.

Staraku stood frozen with her mouth wide open.

"Let me have a look at you," he squinted at her through his little glasses.

Staraku almost laughed with relief. *Why was I afraid of him?* He barely measured up to her chin. Nevertheless, he seemed to fill up the space with his presence. He stood in front of her and smiled back.

"I've been waiting for you."

"What?" Staraku asked. "Then I'm not the one you're looking for. I just decided I was going to land here."

"Oh, I've known for quite a while, Staraku."

She almost choked. "How do you know my name?"

He chuckled and looked toward the ocean. Whether he saw what he was looking for or not, Staraku could not tell. He turned back to her with a shrug.

"Oh, I know a great many things."

Staraku wasn't sure if she liked this little creature or not. Her fear turned to curiosity, and her curiosity into annoyance.

"Who are you anyway?" she asked.

"Agumus."

"Ah-goo-moose," she repeated, sounding it out carefully. "What kind of name is that? I've never heard of it before."

Agumus moved into the shade of the tree, a little closer to Staraku. She took a step back. He found a soft place in the grass that grew right up to the sand, and he sat down. He took off his glasses and rubbed his eyes.

"Well?" Staraku glared at him.

She knew she was being a bit rude, but she was still suspicious of this little guy with the big voice.

He replaced his glasses on his nose and waved his hand in the air. "That is not the most pressing question at hand."

Staraku was mildly offended. "Well, I'd like to know!"

"One should always ask the right questions," he said. "That is, of course, if one wants to get the right answers."

She was about to say something sarcastic, but then he looked deep into her eyes. She tried to look away, but she couldn't because his gaze was magnetic. Kindness glowed and flowed from him. Compassion. No, something more than that. He looked at her as if he knew her quite well—like he really cared about her.

No one has cared about me before. Staraku needed to know more.

"You know who I am?" she asked.

He nodded. "In fact, I may know you better than you know yourself."

Staraku shivered slightly, even though the sun was bright, and the day was warm. She didn't like the idea of this stranger knowing so much about her. No, she didn't like it one bit.

"Come," Agumus invited her, patting the grass beside him. "Come and sit with me. I know you are afraid."

"Yeah, right," Staraku snorted, pretending to be quite brave. She was about to say, "I am not afraid of anyone!" But as she opened her mouth, she realized that she could not lie to this little creature. Not because she didn't want to, but because she realized it was useless. Why lie to someone who already knows the truth? It seemed like he could see right through her. She felt annoyed.

The sand scattered under her as she waddled over to the mound of grass.

She plopped down beside him. "All right, I have a very good question. Why do you want to talk to me if you already know everything?"

He patted her on the wing. "Oh, I don't know the future, only the past," he paused for a moment. "And the present, of course."

She stared at him. "You know everything that has ever happened to me?"

Agumus nodded. "Ah, just the important parts. But only you and your decisions can shape your future."

BUT ONLY YOU AND YOUR DECISIONS CAN SHAPE YOUR FUTURE.

"What are you talking about? What kind of decisions?"

He shook his head and jumped to his feet, which wasn't a very long leap. His legs were very short.

"We mustn't think of that right now. The future has many possibilities." He patted her on the shoulder. "But I have much to teach you, so follow me!"

Staraku stood up. "Hold on, why should I do what *you* say? I just met you!"

He cocked his head and peered over his glasses at her and chuckled. "Do you have other plans?"

"Maybe I do! And even if I didn't, what makes you so confident I want to come with you?" Staraku startled herself as these critical words came out of her own mouth.

He chuckled again and explained.

"Well, I am confident in my purpose. I know who I am and what I was born to do." His now louder voice shook some of the smaller crystals hanging from the tree branch. "I have a special job to do. I help those who are lost."

"I'm not lost," she protested.

"Oh? Where are you then?"

She had nothing to say.

"And you know where you're going, do you?"

"Well, not entirely," she admitted sheepishly.

He smiled and gave a single nod. "Do you even know why you're here on *Crystal Island* of all islands?"

Ah, so that's what this place is called. The way he said it made Staraku feel like there was more to this island than she could see. But instead of asking, she stuck her beak out in defiance. "Actually, I do. I . . . " she hesitated. "I am looking for a friend."

"Oh?" his eyebrows pinched together. "What's your friend's name? Maybe I've seen your friend."

"I'm not looking for a particular friend. Any friend will do."

He shook his head in caution. "Ah, I see. Well, be careful with what you say you want. Especially in this place." He gazed up. "Having a friend isn't always as easy as it looks. Are you ready to be a friend?"

HAVING A FRIEND ISN'T ALWAYS AS
EASY AS IT LOOKS. ARE YOU
READY TO BE A FRIEND?

She was offended. "*I'm* not the problem. I'm a great friend. It's everyone else who is being so difficult."

"So, you are sure you want a friend?"

Her beak shook a little as she admitted, "It's what I've always dreamed of."

Agumus abruptly stood up and bowed to her like she was royalty. "Then let me make an announcement! I am your very first friend!"

Staraku was taken completely by surprise. She simply stared at him with her beak hanging open.

"I thought you'd be a bit more excited having dreamed of this your entire life!" Agumus said, looking up at her.

She paused, and noticing Agumus' frown, explained, "Oh, no. Don't get me wrong. I am thrilled that you are my first friend. Truly, I am!"

Agumus began, "But—"

"Well, I've just never had one before," she admitted. "I never thought about what I'd do when I finally found one!" She got off the ground and hopped around on her bird legs, swinging her body in a little dance.

"So, you're happy?"

"Yes!" she giggled.

"Good!" Agumus lifted off of the ground even though he had no wings. His swishy, sandy cloak flowed behind him. He simply elevated and moved silently into the forest from which he'd earlier appeared. "I have a special gift to give you. Let's go. Come on. Keep up!"

She stood there staring after him. Just as he was about to disappear among the trees, he paused. "Are you coming or not?"

She flapped her wings, jumping off the ground at the same time to give herself a good launch. She flew as quickly as she could, but he was already out of sight before she could catch up to him.

CHAPTER 6

He's certainly not what I expected as my first friend.
Staraku thought to herself as she followed Agumus into the thick island forest. *Can I trust him?* She wasn't sure. But he did say he wanted to give her a gift, and no one had ever given her a gift before. Her curiosity outweighed her doubt and she kept following.

Staraku dipped low to dodge leafy branches and the crystals that hung from them. They buzzed a little as she passed them, as if they were alive. As they flew further into the forest, Staraku smelled the damp, lemony swamp plants below her. She could only see the sky above through teeny slits in the trees. Wherever the sun peeked through, the crystals glimmered.

Agumus screeched to a halt, and Staraku nearly slammed into him. His feet settled back on the ground, soft as flower petals. She flapped as she lost her balance and had to steady herself. "Well, you could have told me we were stopping," she mumbled.

He looked at her with a twinkle in his eyes. "But what's the fun in that?"

She was trying to think of some witty comeback when the crystals dangling overhead caught her attention. On every branch hung dozens of them in all sizes and shapes. "They're so beautiful. Agumus, why are they here?"

Agumus turned to face her. He wanted to make sure she heard him clearly. "They are beautiful, but they're not like any other crystals. They are special."

"Why are they so special? And what kind of island is this, anyway?"

"Crystal Island is a place like no other." He leaned in close and whispered. "It has a secret. Someday you will understand."

"CRYSTAL ISLAND IS A PLACE LIKE NO OTHER." HE LEANED IN CLOSE AND WHISPERED. "IT HAS A SECRET. SOMEDAY YOU WILL UNDERSTAND."

Before she could say another word, he began to rise into the air. "Stay where you are," he instructed.

"Hey, don't go! I want to understand now!" Staraku complained. *And where is my gift?*

If Agumus heard her, he didn't show it. She watched him levitate higher up the trunk of the tree, searching the tree branches. Staraku looked up and up and up, trying to see the top of this massive tree. It was one of the tallest she'd ever seen.

Staraku heard Agumus muttering to himself, "Is that the one?" Then he'd wait for a moment, listening. *What's he listening for?* "No, no, you're right. Maybe this one? No, that's not it."

He moved up higher and higher, searching branch after branch, as if he were receiving directions. Finally, when he was almost to the top, he exclaimed, "This one? Yes. That's it!"

Agumus looked down from far above, waving the crystal over his head. "I found it!" *Swoosh!* He was back on top of the mossy log with a crystal in his hand. He held it up so she could get a good look at it.

"Is this my gift?" Staraku asked.

Agumus nodded, expecting Staraku to be delighted. Instead, she frowned. *My first gift is a rock.* She couldn't hide her disappointment, and blurted out, "It's beautiful, but we're surrounded by these. They're all over the island. Why give me this one?"

He chuckled. "I can see you're going to be a bit more difficult than the others. Yes, there are nearly a gazillion crystals on this island. But trust me, this one is very, very special."

Staraku moved in closer to get a better look. It was shiny and clear, reflecting what little light came through the leaves. "What's so special about it?" She peered into his palm.

"It's special because it is *yours*," he said solemnly. He puffed up his chest as if he were presiding over a great moment in history. He bowed, extended his short arm, and handed her the stone. The moment it touched her hand, the crystal burst with light.

"Oh!" Staraku jumped in fright. "What's happening? Why is it glowing? Is this some kind of a trick?"

A sad look flashed across Agumus' face. "No, no, Staraku. I'm not here to trick you. You can trust me."

Staraku nodded.

Agumus explained. "Every crystal reflects the light when the sun shines through it. But this crystal is glowing because it *belongs* to you. It recognizes you."

Oddly enough, that made sense to Staraku. The crystal fit perfectly in the fold of her wing, as if it was made just for her. Its light bounced off the leaves, lit up the sand, and danced on the water. It made her teal scales shimmer, and it brightened her golden wings. Giving into her growing fascination, she twirled as its light danced over her scales.

Her eyes grew wide. "This is really mine?"

Agumus assured her, "This is your crystal, and it's always been your crystal."

She held it up. The light shined on her face. It added brilliance to all of the gorgeous colors in her feathers, fins, and scales. She looked down at herself with a sense of awe.

"I look . . . different. I look wonderful!" She gasped. She'd never felt wonderful before.

Of course." Agumus nodded like her wonderfulness was obvious.

She walked over to a stream nearby and looked at her reflection. "I've never seen myself like this before."

"Look who's feeling confident now!"

She fumbled for words, feeling somewhat embarrassed. "Well, I-I didn't say—" She stopped and looked up, noticing he was grinning.

He put up his hand to stop her explanation. "You are right to be confident. Being a Birdfish is quite an incredible thing!"

His words caught her off guard. She hesitated to ask the question she'd been wondering. "You-you still want to be my friend even though you know I'm a Birdfish? No one likes a Birdfish."

"Not true, my child. I like you a great deal." He waved his little arm in the air. "And why would I be your very first friend if I didn't? Why would I give you your very first gift if I didn't?"

Staraku had no answers.

He returned to his lesson. "You need to understand light."

"You mean like the sun?" She squinted at him.

He adjusted his short robe. "Yes, like the sun, but the sun isn't with us twenty-four hours a day. When the sun sets, the light is gone." He pointed to the crystal she held. "But *this* type of light *never* goes out. You must take the crystal with you wherever you go."

YOU MUST TAKE THE CRYSTAL WITH YOU WHEREVER YOU GO.

"Why?" Staraku asked.

"The light from your crystal will show you what is in the darkness. You'll be able to see who you can trust and who means you harm."

"And what happens if someone wants to hurt me?"

"That's the magic of it. When you have it with you, it places an invisible line around you. No one can cross it."

Agumus moved closer to her. "How do you feel right now, Staraku?"

She paused and then a smile came to her face. "I feel safe."

"Do you know what happens when you feel safe?"

Staraku shook her head. "Nope."

"When we feel safe, we can be calm. And when we're calm, we're at our best!"

"Yes," Staraku acknowledged. "I do feel the best I've ever felt! Thank you, Agumus. For my gift."

"I have another one for you."

"More?" she was astonished.

"Yes, I want to introduce you to another friend."

Staraku's sense of safety shattered. "Do I have to?"

He looked at her in surprise. "I thought that's what you wanted—to make friends."

Looking down at the sand, she spoke very softly. "No one—well, except for you—has ever liked me."

"You don't have to be afraid, Staraku."

She looked at the crystal. "Because of this?" She wrinkled her beak. "You said it will show me who might be safe or dangerous, but you didn't say it would make everyone like me."

Agumus grinned. "Fair enough." He suddenly clapped his hands and said, "Well, lucky for you, you don't have to meet her right away. I have something

I need to go take care of first. I'll be back before you know it."

"You're leaving?" Staraku felt stung.

Agumus nodded his head. "When I come back, I will take you to meet my friend who lives in the forest. Relax. Enjoy your crystal!"

"But—" she protested.

He then became very serious. "But listen—wait for me. Don't go in alone."

"Where are you going? Why can't I go into the forest alone?" she asked. But there was no answer. He was already gone.

CHAPTER 7

"How rude!" Staraku was furious. She stomped in circles kicking sand as she went. "He just pops in and pops out whenever he wants. Who does he think he is, anyway?"

Plopping onto the ground, she huffed. "Who says I even want to meet anyone? What if they're mean to me? Who needs more of that?"

The more she thought about meeting any one new, the more she began to panic. She fiddled with her crystal. "Ha! What a fool I am. Believing in this silly crystal business? This is just like any other rock on the island!"

She shot upright as a thought struck her. *Maybe he won't come back at all. Maybe it was all too good to be true.* She felt a pang of sadness in her chest. The idea hurt too much to handle.

"I don't even know if I *want* him to come back." She tried to convince herself that was true, jumping to her feet and pacing in circles again.

"I've always been on my own. I've always taken care of myself. I don't need him," Staraku raged out loud, bitter confidence boiling up in her. She looked down at her crystal. "And I don't even need this stupid rock." She looked deep into the forest and threw the crystal as far into the blackness as she could. It went so far that she didn't even hear it land.

Wiping her wings together as if brushing off the dust of her stone, she declared, "I don't need anything to keep me safe. And I don't need to wait for some silly blue creature before I go on my own adventure!" A bad feeling turned in her stomach, but she ignored it.

I'm going into the forest with or without Agumus. She stepped across the line where sand met soil. Instantly, the towering trees dwarfed her tiny body. The dark shadows were big enough to swallow her whole.

* * *

The further she walked, the darker it became. The tall trees above her cut out all direct sunlight, and the crystals hung like dark shards of glass from their branches. When it was quiet, she still thought she could hear them buzzing. Long vines wrapped around the trees, and the damp ground squished beneath her webbed feet. The further she went, the less she could see. In the heat of the afternoon, steam rolled off the trickling water nearby. Hazy sunbeams peeked through the leafy canopy above. Other than that, it became so dark she lost her sense of direction.

Feeling a little less certain, Staraku wished that she still had the crystal with her—just a little bit. She tried to reassure herself. *It's not like I need it… but it might be a good idea to get out of this forest. Back to where I was supposed to wait for Agumus.*

She tried to retrace her steps, but quickly realized it was no use. Every direction looked the same. She was lost. In the dark. Alone, without her crystal. Tears stung her eyes, as she realized that she had let her pride get the best of her. She ran back and forth. She frantically flew one way and then back in the opposite direction. She wished she had waited for Agumus.

> **EVERY DIRECTION LOOKED THE SAME. SHE WAS LOST. IN THE DARK. ALONE, WITHOUT HER CRYSTAL.**

A sense of danger swept over her. "What am I going to do?" She called out "Agumus! Where are you? I'm in here!" But there was no answer. She kept checking whenever she saw a small patch of open sky above her, thinking she might catch a glimpse of him hovering by, but she never did.

She didn't know why, but she had a growing anxiety that something terrible was about to happen. She suspected that's what was bound to happen when someone didn't listen to Agumus. "What have I done?" she cried out as panic overwhelmed her. "The only thing he told me to do was to wait, and I didn't!" She wailed loudly with bitter regret.

Staraku heard a rustling in the leaves and spun around to see what it could be. But she saw nothing that might have caused the sound. Panic caught in her throat, and she screamed. Blinded by darkness and fear, she slammed up and fell against a gargantuan tree. Trying to get her balance, she felt a new surge of anger jolt through her.

"Why did Agumus abandon me?" she said aloud, thinking there was no one there to hear her. She straightened up and saw a little branch sprouting on the giant trunk. It was so much smaller than her. Huffing with anger, she thrust her wing out and snapped the little branch right off the tree.

A horrible ringing filled her head and the whole forest around her. The branch fell from her hand as her wings shot up to cover her ears. The ringing went on and on and on. She'd do anything to make the awful noise stop. It kept up for almost a minute as she leaned frozen at the base of the tree.

Gradually, the sound faded, and she opened her eyes. *What on earth was that?*

Before she could figure it out, she heard the rustling again. "Who—who's there?" she stuttered. It sounded both far and near. It wasn't like footprints, but a low slithering all around her. Puzzled, she scanned the area, including the swaying vines above. *Maybe it's just the wind.*

But then a chilling thought set in. Staraku held up her wing and confirmed it. *There was no wind.* The quiet hiss grew louder, and the vines dropped lower. She squinted her eyes to get a better look, and her heart nearly stopped. *Those aren't vines.*

Emerald tree boas with long, coiling bodies dangled from the trees. They were lime green, with pale scar-like patches along their backs. Their heads were thick, diamond-shaped, with cold, beady eyes. A flash of fangs shone from pale pink mouths.

In that moment, something cold, slick, and strong snapped at her. Fast and silent, before Staraku could take a breath, the snake coiled around her with its vise-like grip. She felt the blood drain from her face. Her beak opened, but no words came out. It held her so tightly and its body was so cold she couldn't even feel her own body anymore.

"Didn't anyone tell you to never come into this forest alone?" The boa hissed. Its voice startled her. For just a moment, it brought her out of her stupor. She tried to speak but could not. *Oh yes, someone did tell me that.* Her vision blurred, and all she could hear was the *hisssss.*

"DIDN'T ANYONE TELL YOU TO NEVER COME INTO THIS FOREST ALONE?" THE BOA HISSED.

The huge snake pulled his head high above hers and opened his terrible mouth. Long, needle-sharp fangs flashed while its tongue flickered down at her. She strained away, struggling for air. The snake hissed at her again. "You foolish, foolish . . ." It paused for a second. "Well, whatever it is that you are—you're a very foolish one. But you'll still taste just fine."

CHAPTER 8

"Staraku!" she heard her name. Through swollen eyes, she saw a fuzzy blue comet speeding toward her. It was Agumus. In his small blue palm was the shining stone—her very own crystal—and it was just the thing she'd been longing to see. But it was hard to breathe. *How did he find me here?* Everything seemed like a hazy dream rippling in and out of her consciousness.

The hissing stopped as the snake was momentarily caught off guard. Its tight grip loosened just a bit.

"Catch!" Agumus bellowed as he threw her crystal to her with a force much stronger than his tiny size would allow.

She tried to pull herself fully free of the snake as it was distracted. She only managed to wiggle one wing from between the its thick folds.

She saw the crystal coming at her and stuck out her wing. *Catch it! Catch it!* It hit her wing and bounced toward the tree. She watched as the glowing stone fell like a star.

Worse yet, in her clumsy attempt to catch the crystal, she threw both herself and the snake off balance. With its long body wrapped around her now, it had no anchor to stop them as they toppled together.

She landed with the full weight of the snake on top of her. Suddenly, she felt a burst of warmth; a sense of calm growing inside her and around her. She realized she had fallen directly on top of the crystal.

A strange thing happened the moment she and the crystal made contact. The stone shone even brighter, allowing her to see the snake's thick body wrapped around her. She turned her head and they stared into each other's eyes for a flickering moment. The snake's tongue slithered in and out of its mouth, smelling her fear. Its mouth opened and was about to devour her with those huge fangs when a flash of light nearly blinded them both.

Staraku's stone sparked and sizzled, and it lit up the entire area. The snake's eyes grew wide with surprise. It froze with its mouth wide open, but Staraku could see its courage draining. She saw it for what it was—a mean creature—and that gave her courage she'd not had before.

The boa turned its face away because the light was too bright for its tiny eyes; it was long used to the darkness of the forest. She freed her wings and beat against its body. Surprised by her strength, the folds of its body uncoiled and rolled back up into the tree. All the other boas in the trees disappeared silently, melting back into a sea of green.

Staraku stood on her feet amazed at how sure of herself she felt. She leaned down and picked up her crystal as it sparkled through the forest night. Its light revealed every small detail of her surroundings she couldn't see before. She felt safe and strong—aglow with all things around her.

All was silent except for the sound of Staraku's own breathing and the *pat pat pat* of Agumus treading toward her over mushed leaves. He came back into focus—his thin-rimmed glasses and round face approaching with concern.

"Oh Staraku." He looked at her with sad eyes.

She sat up and her mind started to clear. She realized what she'd done.

"I-I'm so sorry," she blubbered. "I know you said to wait for you. You warned me not to leave the stone behind—not to leave the light. I didn't realize—"

"I know, I know," he said, his words soothing her.

"And . . . " she hesitated moment, "it's just, well, no one's ever liked me before. I was afraid you were going to leave for good." She shook her head. "I'm sorry. I should have just waited for you."

"I know how hard it can be to trust someone when you've been hurt. I really do." His eyes were very serious behind his tiny frames.

She perked up and raised her crystal into the air as glimmers and flickers of light played against the trees. "But look at me now!"

He smiled. "You learned your lesson, quite the hard way."

Staraku looked sheepish. "I nearly died, didn't I?"

He nodded. "Oh, yes. Without the light, all is darkness."

"I've always been afraid of the dark—even back on my island," she admitted.

"It's not the darkness that is dangerous, my dear. It's what lurks in the darkness. Without the light, you can't see what you are up against. But with the light, you can see who means you harm and stand up for yourself."

WITHOUT THE LIGHT, YOU CAN'T SEE WHAT YOU ARE UP AGAINST. BUT WITH THE LIGHT, YOU CAN SEE WHO MEANS YOU HARM AND STAND UP FOR YOURSELF.

"And I will be able to recognize a friend if I ever meet another one!" Staraku smiled. "I'll never leave my crystal behind again."

Agumus stood silent for a moment, looking up to some distant place. "Wouldn't it be so much easier if we'd known about the light from the start?"

Staraku wondered what Agumus' life was like before he found his light.

"But once you do find the light, you never forget." Agumus smiled at the little crystal as if he was thanking it.

Staraku looked down at it again, a glimmering little mystery.

"Agumus, how did it *do* that? And what kind of island is this?" she asked. She suspected this small stone and this whole island were even more than Agumus had described.

"I told you, Crystal Island isn't just any island. And that isn't just any stone. You will see things here that you never dreamed were possible."

She tried to understand. There he went again, talking about how this "isn't just any island." But he still never answered her—*what kind of island is this?*

Before she could form another question, he wiped his hands together and said, "Well, I think that's enough for one day."

Staraku couldn't argue. It had been an extremely long day.

"Follow me out of this forest, and we'll return tomorrow to meet my friend."

Agumus floated up to lead the way, and Staraku happily flew behind him. Once they reached the forest's edge, they landed.

Staraku asked, "Do you think it could be possible that your friend would want to be friends with me?" She was hoping that he would say yes.

He cocked his head to the side and gave it some thought. "I can't guarantee it, but there's a chance."

"Why can't you guarantee it?" Staraku whined. "Then what's the point?"

He sighed. "Wait for me here tomorrow. I promise I will come. You won't want to meet my friend without me being there."

"Why?"

And once again, he disappeared.

CHAPTER 9

The sun was up again before she had awakened. "Wake up!" Agumus peered down into Staraku's sleeping face.

She yawned and stretched. "Give me a second."

"Not a second to spare," he called over his shoulder as he floated toward the forest.

"Hey, wait!" Staraku shouted after him, but it was no use. He was already out of hearing distance. She took to the air and flew after him. *He may be my first friend, but he can be very irritating.*

When she caught up with him, Agumus was standing on a rock. He was chattering in the distance, seemingly to no one. When she approached him, he waved his arms high above his head, as if presenting something. It all seemed so strange. Staraku wondered if she was dreaming.

"Umm, what are you doing?" she asked, scanning the area.

"I have someone for you to meet!"

Staraku looked around. "Who? We're alone in the forest." But as soon as she said it, she wasn't so sure.

"No, no. Staraku, I think you're ready to learn that we are not alone at all."

Her eyes followed where his hands were pointing. "All I see is a tree." She stood there puzzled.

"Exactly," he said. "This is my friend."

She scrunched up her face. "Okay, the joking is over. Who am I really going to meet today?"

He turned away to face the tree again. The tree swayed lightly.

Staraku waddled up onto the rock Agumus had stood on to elevate himself. "Oh no, you're serious, aren't you?"

He was still gazing upward, as if the answer was clear. He motioned upward. "This is Rutuma."

"A tree?"

"Yes, a tree."

"Okay, I'll go along with the joke. Hello, Rutuma, the tree. How are you today?" Staraku was clearly annoyed. "Ah, no answer? You know why, Agumus? Because trees don't talk."

"You could hear her if you truly wanted to."

She sighed and folder her wings across her scaled chest.

"Rutuma does talk. Ignore the ears on the sides of your head. They're of no use hearing her. But if you open your inner ears, you will hear Rutuma clearly. It will take a little practice, but you'll get the hang of it."

Staraku shook her head. "I don't know how to do that. I don't have any other ears."

"Actually, Staraku, you already know how to hear her voice. Where were you standing when the boa grabbed you last night?"

She looked around for a moment, then her eyes shot open wide. "Is this the same place where that happened?" She whipped her head around. She almost didn't recognize it in the daylight. "You brought me back here?!" Staraku protested as Agumus waved his small hands to quiet her.

"Calm yourself, Staraku. You have your crystal with you, don't you?"

She pulled it out from under her wing.

"Okay then. Take a few deep breaths," he instructed her. "I am introducing you to Rutuma because you have some unfinished business here."

She was puzzled. But as her eyes moved up the giant tree, she saw a tiny bare spot—a spot where a little branch had started to grow before being torn off. Suddenly Staraku knew exactly which tree this was. She could almost still feel the tiny green sprout snap in her wing.

"Did you notice anything after you broke her branch?" Agumus prodded.

"Before the snake ambushed me? Not really." But then it hit her. "The ringing sound. It was horrible! Like a scream." Her beak dropped open. "Was that *her*?"

Agumus nodded.

"Oh, no," Staraku whispered. "Did I hurt her?"

With a clear, transcending voice that surprised Staraku, the tree responded, "Yes, Staraku. In your fear, you hurt me."

Staraku heard the words as clear as the whistling wind or the creaking limbs, but in a way that bypassed all her senses and went straight to her soul.

Staraku stammered. "B-but I've n-never hurt anyone in my life!"

"Ah, but you have. You ended the life of a young shoot." The tree spoke straight to Staraku's core.

Staraku looked down at the branch lying lifeless on the ground. She whimpered. "I didn't mean to—"

"That's nearly always how it happens."

Agumus agreed. "There are those who are cruel deep in their hearts. They don't care if they hurt others. But most of us just get caught up in our fear or anger. When we do that, we usually hurt someone—even if we don't mean to. "

Staraku felt terrible. Her lower beak began to quiver so badly she feared she might start to cry. At that moment her crystal shone with a burst of brilliant light. In the flash, she realized the truth.

She took a deep breath and turned toward Rutuma. "I did mean to break it off. I was frustrated, but I just didn't know that it—or you—would be hurt." Staraku remembered herself being bitten in the ocean and chased in the sky. *Did the birds and the fish realize how much pain they caused me?*

Agumus nodded. "Every living creature has its own feelings, fears, and dreams. Sometimes, we just don't recognize it."

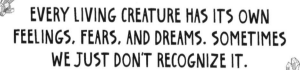

EVERY LIVING CREATURE HAS ITS OWN FEELINGS, FEARS, AND DREAMS. SOMETIMES WE JUST DON'T RECOGNIZE IT.

Rutuma sighed. "This branch could have grown strong and tall. It could have carried many crystals until their owners arrived. Everything has its own life, Staraku—its own purpose."

Staraku looked up. "I definitely never thought about what it could have grown into."

Rutuma whispered with unexpected softness. "I know, I know."

Staraku's stomach tensed, and she furrowed her brow. It was a horrible idea that she was pondering—that when she was hurt, she often hurt others without realizing it. Finally, with her new courage, she stood up and declared with her whole heart what she knew was the truth. "I realize that I hurt you, Rutuma."

The tree whispered in Staraku's heart. "Thank you. That's very brave. It's hard to be honest. There are many who make excuses instead."

"I don't feel very good," Staraku confessed. "Is this what honesty feels like? If so, I hate it."

Agumus snickered, "No, Staraku. That's what *guilt* feels like, but it doesn't have to last forever. You can make it go away."

"How?"

"Let me ask you this, Staraku. What do you wish would happen when someone hurts you?"

She thought for a moment. "That they'd apologize."

He smiled and then tilted his head toward Rutuma.

Staraku said to Rutuma, meaning every word, "I am very sorry."

Suddenly, a small droplet of water fell onto the top of Staraku's head. She opened her eyes, looked up, and realized that the tree had cried a single tear.

"Your apology is accepted," Rutuma said.

All the tension in Staraku's body melted into relief.

"With forgiveness comes the possibility of friendship," Agumus said. "Your crystal has shown you this truth."

WITH FORGIVENESS COMES THE POSSIBILITY OF FRIENDSHIP.

Staraku gazed down on the glowing stone. "Yes, I learned that when I make mistakes, I can apologize." Staraku smiled brightly. "Hey, I feel better! I feel so free! So light."

Agumus laughed. "That's what forgiveness feels like! That's how you know your heart is pure."

Staraku somehow knew Rutuma was smiling from branch to branch.

"I am delighted to be your friend," Rutuma declared.

Staraku gasped. "You're willing to be my friend after I hurt you?"

"Oh, I've always been willing to be your friend," Rutuma said. The tree looked down at Agumus. "Did you tell her I might not be willing to be her friend?"

Agumus dragged his toe through the wet dirt. "Well, maybe."

Rutuma said, "Come here, Staraku."

Staraku leaned against Rutuma's smooth bark and shared a hug with her second ever friend.

"I get it now," Staraku beamed.

"Get what?" Agumus looked at her with curiosity.

"I figured out what makes this island so special now! Why it's not like other islands."

Agumus cocked his head. *Had she really?* He doubted it.

"Yes, of course! This island is special because it's home of Rutuma, the one and only talking tree."

He and Rutuma exchanged a look.

Agumus said, "No, that's not it."

Staraku folded her wings across her chest and insisted, "What could make this island special more than a talking tree?"

Agumus smiled. "That's the next surprise I have for you."

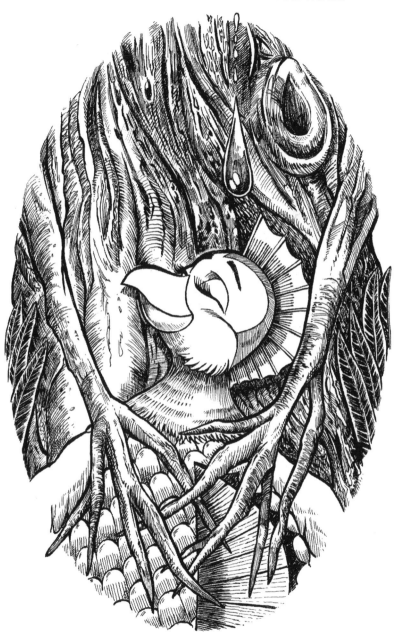

CHAPTER 10

Suddenly all the trees started swaying even though there was no breeze. The crystals rocked back and forth, creating a beautiful melody of chimes and tinkles and joy. It was the most magical music Staraku had ever heard. Agumus spread out his little arms as wide as they could go, and he said, "I'm pleased to introduce you to the forest!"

Staraku held her breath. "Do you mean that every tree around us can talk like you can, Rutuma?"

"Yes. Every living thing talks in its own way. Each has its own different language. We trees have ours. We take in your presence from the soil and sense your vibrations through your heartbeat. We hear the things you want to say but haven't found the words for."

Staraku backed up a little. "Wait a minute. I know that you can talk, but can you also read my mind?"

Agumus cut in. "It's not like that, Staraku. It's much more important than that. They can read your heart. It's much wiser than your mind."

"What if I don't want anyone to read my mind or my heart?"

Agumus smiled. "Nothing you can do to stop that. They know what's in every creature's heart. So much effort goes into hiding what we really feel, what we love and hate, and our deepest longings. But trees see through all of that pretending. They simply know."

Staraku felt very exposed. "I don't want a bunch of trees knowing my secrets." Wanting to hide, she ducked behind the nearest trunk.

"Staraku? You realize you're hiding behind a tree, right?"

Staraku blushed. He was right. She darted out and hid herself beneath a thick leaf, five times her size.

"That leaf is from a tree, my dear." Agumus' voice followed her.

Staraku shook her head and then flew upward into the thick canopy above for privacy.

"Starakuuuu," Agumus' voice bounced around the forest. "You're still in a tree."

"Ugh!" she cried out in exasperation from a high branch. "There's no place to hide in this forest!" She flitted back down to where Agumus stood.

"Let me ask you a question," he said quietly. "When you felt very lonely and scared, back on your island, where did you go?"

Staraku thought about it for a moment and then her eyes got wide. "I flew over the mountains and into the forest."

Agumus nodded. "Yes, and there's a reason for that, Staraku. It's the one place on your island you felt truly safe."

Rutuma explained, "You felt safe in the forest because you *were* safe."

She looked puzzled.

"The trees were protecting you, Staraku," Agumus said.

"Why would they do that?" she asked.

"Because they were your friends. They understood how you felt."

Staraku's eyes grew wide. "Do you mean I had friends back on my island?"

Agumus nodded. "You just didn't know it. And you have friends here, too."

A small smile came to Staraku's beak. *The trees already know how I feel, and they still want to meet me.*

Rutuma said, "Staraku, I'd like to introduce you to my dear friend Kerine."

"Good to meet you," Kerine whispered. She was the one with the willowy branches and light green leaves.

"It's good to meet you too," Staraku whispered back. In her heart, she could hear the trees around giggling and enjoying her newfound joy.

"Let me introduce myself," said the tallest tree in the bunch. "I'm Landerall."

One of the smallest trees shouted out, "Hey, don't forget about me! I'm Nimara!"

One after another, the trees introduced themselves. Staraku grinned brightly.

Landerall chuckled. "I have a very important question to ask our new friend."

"Yes?" they all said in unison as they leaned in closer.

"What is it like to be a Birdfish?"

Staraku was delighted. "No one has ever asked me what it's like to be a Birdfish before!"

Landerall said, "What I really want to know is how does it feel to fly?"

Staraku paused and thought a moment. "What does flying feel like? Well, kind of like your tallest leaves blowing around your branches on a windy day. You feel the wind lift you off and move you forward. Everything below you becomes really small."

"Incredible!" They all marveled together.

"And what does swimming feel like?" Kerine asked.

"Like a rainstorm! But all around you. Everything gets *sooooo* quiet—you can hear your own heartbeat."

The trees were fascinated, and it made her stand a little taller. *It's pretty cool that I can fly and swim. Maybe it's not so bad to be a Birdfish.*

"Do you miss your island?" Nimara asked.

Staraku became very quiet.

"I would miss my friends if I left this island. Don't you miss yours?" the little tree asked softly.

"Shh!" one of the trees warned.

"Why did you ask her that question?" Landerall scolded.

For a moment, all of the trees grew quiet.

"I'm sorry," the tree whispered to her, realizing what she'd done.

"I feel your pain," said another.

Staraku looked up in amazement. "It's hard to imagine anyone knows how I feel."

The tallest tree nodded, shaking his leaves. "When you care about someone, you can feel what they feel."

WHEN YOU CARE ABOUT SOMEONE, YOU CAN FEEL WHAT THEY FEEL.

Staraku confessed, "If I had met the trees on my island, maybe I would miss them. But I don't miss my island now. The fish and the birds didn't like me because I was different."

"What's wrong with being different?" the little tree asked.

"There's nothing at all wrong with that!" Kerine insisted. "How *boring* it would be if everyone was exactly the same."

Landerall agreed. "That's why we like to hear your stories, Staraku. Because you are different!"

Agumus jumped in to help change the mood. "Staraku has a lot of funny and interesting stories," he said. "Staraku, why don't you tell them the story about the time you tried to disguise yourself as a bird!"

Staraku smiled once again. "Oh, that is a funny story. At least it is *now!*" She launched into the tale of the ferns and the sap. She told them how she got caught by trying to help Tori, the bird who didn't stand up for her. "I must have looked so silly! Now, that seems so ridiculous—trying to fit in with creatures who don't . . . " she tried to find the right words.

Agumus offered some help. "Creatures who don't respect you?"

"Yes, that's it!"

One of the trees bowed ever so slightly, and said, "We respect you."

Ahh, respect. That's what I feel now. Staraku smiled. "And that's why I don't miss my island and why I am never going to leave this island. Never, ever, ever!"

They asked her more questions, and she told them more of her stories—how she'd tried to hide from the birds and the fish, but they found her anyway; how she met Agumus and learned about the light. They laughed for hours together. Staraku couldn't remember a time when she had more fun.

And they kept listening when she told the story about the snake, even though all of them had been there when it happened. In fact, when she told that particular tale, they acted like they'd never heard the story before. *That's what friends do*—they agreed silently among themselves. *They listen to others' stories, even if it's the hundredth time they've heard it.*

After a while, Agumus floated back over to Rutuma, landing gently on one of her branches. "It's so nice to see her happy," Agumus said.

Rutuma smiled. "I think this has been the best day of her life."

"I think she's ready to learn the secret of Crystal Island," Agumus confided.

Rutuma agreed. "But first everyone needs a good night's sleep." In a louder tree-voice, Rutuma announced that it was bedtime and since most everyone was yawning, they knew it was true. "Staraku, do you want to spend the night here with us?"

"Oh yes!"

"Well, I'll be off then," Agumus said, and he disappeared immediately.

Rutuma looked down at Staraku. "It's a little irritating when he does that, isn't it?'

Staraku laughed. "You mean when he leaves abruptly without saying a proper goodbye?"

The two friends smiled at each other, knowing they wouldn't want Agumus to be any other way. But behind Rutuma's smile, she held a small seed of worry. There had been many before who didn't have the courage to face the island's secret. She hoped Staraku was ready for what tomorrow would hold.

CHAPTER 11

The next morning Staraku asked Rutuma, "Do you have any idea when Agumus will be here today?"

"He'll be here when it's time," the tree assured her. But Rutuma knew that Agumus was staying away for a reason. It was time to tell Staraku about the secret of Crystal Island, and he always got nervous at this part. Many who had gotten this far turned and went back home after learning the secret.

Rutuma started the conversation with a question. "Have you ever wondered why there are crystals hanging from all of our branches?"

"Yes, I have. Why do you carry them? Aren't they heavy?"

Rutuma laughed as the crystals tinkled and sparkled from her branching arms. "It's what I was created to do, Staraku."

Staraku looked startled. "You're *supposed* to let them hang from you?"

"Yes, it's my purpose." Pointing her branches to the trees around her, she said, "Actually, it's time you learn more about this island. About us"—she motioned to the other trees—"and about why you're here."

Finally, I'm getting some answers. Though something in Staraku wasn't sure she wanted to hear them.

"We trees are the Keepers of the Crystals. It's our job to take care of them until their owners arrive."

"Their owners? Do you mean every single one?"

"Yes, every single crystal has an owner. For every crystal you see here, there is someone out there who feels lost. Scared. Alone. Like they don't belong."

Staraku took in all the crystals around her with a new sense of awe. "Just like me? There are *this* many creatures out there who feel like I did? I thought I was the only one in the world who felt like that."

THERE ARE THIS MANY CREATURES OUT THERE WHO FEEL LIKE I DID? I THOUGHT I WAS THE ONLY ONE IN THE WORLD WHO FELT LIKE THAT.

"Staraku, there's no one else exactly like you. But there are plenty who feel what you have felt."

"Why we do we all have crystals? To keep us safe from bullies?"

"It's not just that, Staraku. That's one small part of what the crystal does. Do you know what it's really for? Your crystal shows you your *purpose*."

"My purpose? What does that mean?"

Rutuma thought for a moment. "Well, your purpose is what *only you can do*. It's why you were made the way you are. Take us trees, for example. We were made to grow strong and tall so we could carry the crystals and give millions of creatures a home in our trunks and branches. As a matter of fact, your crystal appeared on my branch the moment you came into existence, and I kept it for you until you came at just the right time."

Suddenly, Staraku felt hurt. Anger filled up her throat. "Rutuma, that can't be true. I don't have a purpose. I mean, look at me! I'm a Birdfish! I'm a freak of nature. Half this and half that." She looked down at her webbed toes and barely audibly said, "I am a colossal mistake.

"There's no one else like me," she said with tears in her eyes. "I'm all alone. I didn't come here looking for my crystal. I didn't even know I had a crystal. I just wanted to get as far away from my island as possible and—"

"I know, you were looking for a friend." Rutuma said. "But you didn't arrive here by accident. You were *meant* to come to Crystal Island so that you could find your crystal—and more importantly, your purpose."

"Staraku, listen." Rutuma's voice grew louder with authority. "You think you don't have a purpose just because you're different? You couldn't be more wrong!

That's exactly what your crystal wants to show you. Your purpose is found in what makes you *different*. What makes you *different* gives you your power. You can do things no one else can do. Don't you ever call that a mistake, ever again."

> YOUR PURPOSE IS FOUND IN WHAT MAKES YOU DIFFERENT. WHAT MAKES YOU DIFFERENT GIVES YOU YOUR POWER.

Staraku wiped tears from her feathery cheeks. *Could Rutuma's words be true? Could there be any reason I was made this way?*

Rutuma's voice went soft again. "And when you find your purpose, it will be a gift to the world. A gift that only you can give."

"I hope you're right," Staraku whispered.

Just as Rutuma was about to respond, the whole tree began to shake powerfully. A loud moan came up from her roots, shuddered through the trunk, and blasted out the ends of her branches. Staraku covered her ears with her wings trying to block out the horrible sound. Still, it echoed through her heart and body. Like the night Staraku broke the branch, it seemed like the agony went on forever.

"What was that?" Staraku called out.

Agumus appeared with a bang. "Rutuma! Rutuma! The other trees just told me. I came the instant I heard!"

He threw his arms around the tree, and then backed away and paced back and forth across the soft forest floor. Rutuma bent over, as if the crystals were suddenly weighing her down. Staraku had never seen either of them so upset.

"What is going on?" Staraku asked with a shake to her voice.

"I just heard from other trees on another island. They're in trouble," Rutuma said in distress.

"You can hear trees on other islands?" Staraku's eyes were wide.

"Yes," Rutuma nodded seriously. "Usually, we only hear the trees on our own island. But when a forest is desperate, they can send signals to other islands for help."

"How can you help them from here?" Staraku asked.

"Staraku, they're not asking for my help. They're asking for *you*. It's *your* island. The trees on your island are in terrible danger."

Staraku felt numb. *How can the trees on my island know I'm here? What could be happening to them right now?*

"The trees n-need *me*?" she stuttered.

Rutuma nodded sharply. "Not just the trees. The whole island needs you, especially the birds and the fish. They say there's not much time."

Staraku narrowed her eyes in disbelief. Her mind was filled with scenes of the birds and fish tormenting her. "Why should I help them?" Staraku's eyes flared. She turned abruptly and shot a look at Agumus. "And don't to try to talk me into going back!" Staraku was livid.

But Agumus' face was soft. "No, Staraku, you don't have to go."

"But they hate me! And they never helped me when I—," Staraku stopped raging. "Wait, did you say I don't have to go?" She looked stunned.

"No, Staraku, you don't." His eyes pierced her with his intense compassion. "You are right. They didn't help you when you needed it. You don't owe it to them."

Staraku looked to Rutuma for support. "See Rutuma? They don't deserve my help. And I don't have to go."

"If I were in trouble, would you be willing to help me?" Rutuma asked softly.

That question stopped Staraku short. "Of course, I would. I would do anything for you. But you're my friend."

"What about helping a friend of a friend? Someone just like me who is in serious danger?" Rutuma asked.

All of the trees leaned in at that moment, eager to hear Staraku's answer.

80

CHAPTER 12

Staraku looked over to Agumus, and said, "So this is what you meant by sometimes friendship doesn't turn out like I might expect."

Agumus nodded. "Sometimes friendship means helping when it's not convenient, or pleasant, or even safe. But you do not have to go. It's your choice to give this gift."

SOMETIMES FRIENDSHIP MEANS HELPING WHEN IT'S NOT CONVENIENT, OR PLEASANT, OR EVEN SAFE.

A gift? Staraku remembered what Rutuma had said. A bright flicker caught her eye and she realized that her crystal was glowing brighter through her wing feathers.

"If you do, though, it is not because they deserve it, but because you actually want to help." Agumus paused before continuing. "What will you do?"

As he asked her, all the images of her old bullies disappeared. In their place, all she could see was the small branch she tore and Rutuma—who forgave her.

"I don't care about the birds and the fish," Staraku declared honestly. "But I will go back to help the trees. I don't want any of the trees to suffer." She turned to Agumus. "Will you come with me?"

"Of course," Agumus said. His eyes were gleaming.

"Wait," Rutuma said, "Will you give me your crystal?"

Staraku threw a surprised glance at Agumus, who shrugged his shoulders. She put her crystal into an outstretched branch. In another branch, Rutuma held a slender vine, and she slipped it around the crystal, tying a strong knot that held the stone secure.

"Please turn around," Rutuma instructed. Staraku did, and Rutuma gently tied the vine at the back of her neck.

Staraku turned back with a broad smile and a crystal necklace like none she'd ever seen.

"Now, you will always have the light in front of you, wherever you go."

Staraku leaned forward and placed her wings tightly around Rutuma's trunk. "Thank you, my friend," she whispered.

Rutuma whispered back, "I am the one who is most grateful."

Agumus nodded to Rutuma and then he and Staraku rose straight into the air. Rutuma watched them until they disappeared into the sky. She wondered if they'd get there in time.

The two friends flew faster than they ever thought they could. Before the island came into view, they spied a large dark cloud in the distance. As they approached, the large plume of smoke rose higher in the sky, making it difficult to see the island below. Staraku wondered if the entire island must be ablaze to fill the sky with such darkness.

Agumus with his natural glow and Staraku wearing her radiant crystal dove down into the billows, but the smoke was so thick their light didn't help much. Breaking through the smoky cloud, they landed on the lagoon in a circle of trees.

The tallest tree cried out with relief to the trees around him. "Rutuma heard us! They're here!"

Shouts of joy rippled through the forest, but they were interrupted by a blinding flash of lightning that lit up the entire sky. A moment later, the *BOOM* of thunder shook the island to its core.

"How did this happen?" Staraku's voice cracked with fear as she looked up at the big tree.

"It's a dry thunderstorm," the tree explained. "It's when thunder and lightning strikes, but the rain dries before it reaches the ground. The lightning starts the fires, but there's no rain to put it out."

"Where are the birds and fish?" Agumus raised his voice over the sound of fire crackling. It burned hot and spread quickly. The smell of smoke was inescapable.

The tree was clearly disappointed. "Well, we're holding their nests as tightly as we can, and we're trying to cover the eggs in the water from ash. But they're off doing what they always do—fighting. They're too caught up in who started the fire to bother putting it out."

Staraku and Agumus followed his limb as he pointed to The Rock. That's when they noticed the yelling.

Agumus lifted off of the sand. "Come on, Staraku. Let's go."

The ocean bubbled with white froth. It was total chaos.

The birds screeched, "Take that, you slimy fish! This is your fault!" They hurled rocks into the ocean with large splashes.

The fish leapt out from the water in rage, hollering with fury. "You're the one to blame for this fire. Not us! We'll get you soaking wet. You'll fall into the ocean and drown!"

Hovering above the madness, Agumus put his tiny arms up on Staraku's shoulders. "You've got to talk to them. The fire is heading straight for the grove of trees surrounding the lagoon. If we don't do something quick, the trees and the baby birds will die. If the trees go down, they'll fall straight into the lagoon and crush the fish eggs."

Staraku shot a wild look at Agumus. "Are you crazy? They hated me even before all this! I'll be attacked by both sides!"

"But you have your crystal. Have you lost faith?"

"I have my crystal. I just—I'm the wrong one for this job. The trees should have sent for someone else."

Agumus gave her a quiet, steady look. "Staraku, you speak all three languages. You speak fish, you speak bird, and you speak tree. You can unite the island and put out this fire before anyone gets hurt. Who else can do that?"

Rutuma's words rung back in Staraku's mind: *You were made the way you are for a reason.*

YOU WERE MADE THE WAY YOU ARE FOR A REASON.

Turning to Agumus, she voiced her fears. "But even if I could get them to follow me, I have no plan. How could a bunch of birds and fish put out a fire of any size, let alone one that is consuming the entire island?"

Agumus put his hand to his chin and looked up in the sky, as if somewhere in the smoky clouds he'd find an answer. "The answer is this: if you all use your strengths together, you can do something amazing that has never been done before."

Staraku still felt afraid, but the crystal glowed even brighter filling her with a new sense of hope. She carefully considered his words. "If you all use your strengths together . . . " She looked straight at him as a new thought sparked in her mind. "I've got an idea!" Without another word, she spread her wings and flew directly into the battle.

CHAPTER 13

As she flew down and landed on The Rock, right between the birds and fish. Staraku expected everyone to join together and attack her. But

instead, the birds who were about to drop rocks froze at the sight of her. Fish rose to the surface with their mouths full of water only to stare at Staraku as the water ran down their chins. All eyes landed on her with a mix of fear and wonder. Then they all started to babble at once.

"Is that the Birdfish?" one fish asked.

"What's that around her neck?" a bird squawked.

"It looks like she's glowing," another bird added.

"She's back for revenge!"

"After what we did to her, she'll kill us!"

Panic spread through the crowds faster than the fire was ravaging the island beyond them. *They're afraid of me!* Staraku put up her wing, and they stopped.

Staraku spoke directly to the birds and the fish in their own languages. "You don't need to be afraid of me. You need to be afraid of what the fire can do to your island if you keep fighting like this!"

Gaining a little confidence, one of the birds yelled out, "Don't listen to her! She's just a crazy Birdfish!" The birds and fish burst out laughing. Their laughter stung.

Fear rippled through her body. She squeezed her crystal with her wing.

"I'm not running away again," she declared through her clenched beak. When she said it, her crystal glowed so brightly that the birds and fish shielded their eyes with their wings and fins. They stopped laughing then.

Pointing to the island she shouted, "Look!" Everyone's eyes turned to the yellow and orange flames dancing toward the lagoon. "Do you see where the fire is headed?" Finally, they did.

"It's headed for the lagoon!" one of the birds declared.

"Oh, no! My babies are up there in those trees!" cried one of the mother birds.

The fish looked across the ocean. "What if those trees fall?" asked one of the fish.

"We won't be able to get to our eggs," a mother fish cried in horror.

"The fire is moving so fast!" one bird shrieked.

"Our homes! They're going to burn if we don't do something!"

At that moment, another fiery bolt of lightning struck the dry grass closer to the lagoon, and a new fire burst into life. A clap of thunder bellowed across the island a moment later. The leaves shook, and the air grew even smokier. Birds scattered and fish shot underwater for cover. Staraku heard the cries for help coming from the trees.

Staraku flew above them. "I have a plan, but we all have to work together!" she screamed out in both languages. "Follow me!" she shouted to the fish, and she plunged into the murky grey water. But when she turned around, she was alone. They cowered under water in clusters against The Rock. Staraku realized they weren't just selfish; they were terrified.

She went on without them. She sped down and chewed off a large thick strand of seaweed. She dragged them to the surface with all her might. The wet green leaves trailed behind her. She broke through the surface and into the air, passing the birds. She yelled, "Follow me!" but again, none of them did. They were too afraid.

Agumus met her in the air as Staraku dropped the wet seaweed on top of the fire. The seaweed sizzled sound as it smothered the flames.

She yelled in triumph, "It'll work!"

Agumus landed beside her. "That's a great idea!"

Staraku smiled with hope, but it quickly faded. "I guess you and I will have to do it alone."

Agumus nodded his head, but there was deep concern in his eyes. "Go ahead and get more seaweed, Staraku. I'll meet you at the kelp bed."

Staraku flew through the smoke toward The Rock. *If only I could convince even one of them to help. But how?* Just then, an unexpected voice came through the smoke behind her. The voice was tinged with both fear and uncertainty.

"Staraku?"

A bird was flying by her side. It was Tori, the bird who tormented her mercilessly. The bird who had mocked her and made her cry so many times. A jolt of fear shuddered through Staraku. *Will Tori try to hurt me again?*

Tori looked impressed. "Dropping seaweed on the fire is genius! And you helped me when I needed it. Tell me what I can do. I want to help save my island."

Of all of the birds, I never thought Tori would ever help! Aloud, Staraku yelled, "Fly with me to the where the seaweed kelp beds grow. Then circle the area and wait for me at the surface." Staraku and Tori flew to the spot, and Agumus' face lit up when he saw Tori arrive.

Staraku dove under the surface and began cutting thick, wet strands of glassy kelp. Against the water's current, she swam it back up to the surface, clutching as many strands as she could fit in her beak. Once back at the surface, Tori and Agumus snatched them up and flew as fast as they could to drop them on the flames. The seaweed was so thick and wet, it put out the fire with a loud sizzle wherever it landed.

When she met Tori and Agumus at the surface, Tori cried out, "We need more. We're not going to beat the fire in time!"

Handing off what she had, Staraku yelled back, "This is the fastest I can go!" Staraku dove back down. *How can I do this by myself? We're not going to make it!*

HOW CAN I DO THIS BY MYSELF? WE'RE NOT GOING TO MAKE IT!

"You need more seaweed?" a fish asked. "I want to help."

The fish swimming by her side was Buntu, the one who had led all the fish to her secret hiding places. The one who told her over and over she didn't belong.

Staraku slowed down and looked at him warily.

"I know I've been awful to you," Buntu said. "It makes sense you wouldn't trust me. But my nieces and nephews are in the lagoon. I'll do anything to help them."

Of all of the fish, I never thought Buntu would care about anyone but himself! Aloud, she yelled, "Follow me to the kelp bed."

Buntu hesitated.

Oh, no. He's changed his mind.

Buntu pointed his fin behind him. "When I realized you had a plan that would actually work, I recruited a few friends."

Through the cloudy grey water, Staraku saw hundreds of fish swimming up behind Buntu. A surge of hope shot through Staraku. She remembered Agumus' words, "...if you all use your strengths together..."

"Go get as much kelp as you can and take it to the surface," Staraku yelled. She swam among the fish, showing them the best way to cut the seaweed. She grabbed a load and sped to the surface. The other fish rushed upward alongside of her to help save their fish eggs, the bird nests, and the trees. Staraku felt like she actually swam faster with the current of fish now by her side.

When she broke through the surface of the water, not only were Agumus and Tori waiting for her, but soaring above was the entire flock—even some strange-looking birds she had never seen before. Tori smiled. "I thought we could use some more help!"

Staraku looked over at Agumus who seemed to know exactly what she was thinking. Agumus turned to the birds. "Take the seaweed from the fish as they reach the surface. Fly single file." He sped off toward the island. Over his shoulder, he hollered, "And meet me at the island! I'll show you where to drop the seaweed!"

The fish made dozens of trips down into the depths, cutting and carrying kelp from ocean floor to the surface. The birds flew in formation, each taking seaweed from the next fish in line and flew quickly back to the fire.

At the island, Agumus hovered above the flames, dodging ribbons of smoke and showing the birds where to drop their loads. No one seemed to mind following the directions of a little blue creature who could hover, rather than fly.

The process seemed to go on forever. Staraku lost track of time. They dashed into the depths and erupted to the surface with urgency. But later in the afternoon, as she and the fish broke the surface, there were no birds.

"What's happened?" one of the fish yelled out.

"Did the birds get caught in the fire?" another asked.

"Oh, no!" Staraku gasped. She flew into the air to get a better look. It was hard to see through the smoke. Her eyes searched the shoreline for the glow of her dearest friend. She scanned the smoky sky for the sight of flapping wings.

Tears filled her eyes. Total dread twisted inside of her. But as she broke clear of the smoke, she saw them. The entire flock standing on the shore, necks craned upwards. Agumus hovered above them. *Why aren't they flying anymore?* For a moment, Staraku felt like her heart stopped. *Were we too late?*

CHAPTER 14

Searching for the coral-colored flames behind the birds and below Agumus, she saw a scorched island, but not one flicker of fire. Everywhere she looked, all she could find were pillars of smoke billowing above the shore like kites in the wind.

Bubbling up beside her, other fish rose to the surface with more fresh kelp for the fires. Their wide eyes scanned the still island, the smoky sky, and the silent birds. The kelp dropped from their mouths.

Suddenly, they heard the baby birds start chirping from their nests. The most pure, genuine, and joyful sound filled the gray air. Agumus turned and smiled at Staraku, eyes brimming with tears. He hovered above the crowd and officially declared, "We did it!"

* * *

The birds hugged each other with delight. The fish spun around each other in a dance of joy. And then, as if they had all received a secret signal, they all gushed in unison, "Our babies!" The fish sped through and around the lagoon to the small opening, heading to where they had hidden their eggs. No one could tell if the fish were crying tears of joy—their eyes were wet anyway—but there were huge smiles on all of their faces.

Simultaneously, the birds flew toward the grove and to the tree that housed their nests. The tree branches were dotted with ash but definitely green and vibrant. The high nests in their branches were intact. Mother birds cried and hugged their eggs and baby birds. Fathers slapped each other on the back in mutual celebration of their amazing feat.

Staraku and Agumus stood quietly to the side of the trees, who were quite loud in their celebration.

"You saved us!" the big tree declared.

"We knew you could do it!" another tree sang out.

"Someone has to tell Rutuma that we are safe and that Staraku saved the island!"

The trees swayed together and sang in beautiful harmony of joy and gratitude. Agumus and Staraku could hear their songs.

Both the birds and the fish yelled out, "Thank you! Thank you!"

"Maybe you're not so bad after all!"

"You helped save our babies!"

But neither side understood exactly what the other was saying.

Staraku walked to the water's edge. "Let me translate so you can finally understand each other."

Tori stood at Staraku's side and declared, "On behalf of the birds, we want to thank you fish for helping to save our island, and, of course, our families." The birds squawked and whistled and tweeted in agreement.

Staraku translated, and the fish flapped their fins to show they were delighted.

Buntu swam close to shore. "On behalf of the fish, we want to thank you birds for helping save our families and our island." The fish squirted water into the air and splashed and danced on the water.

Staraku translated, and the birds all tweeted to show they were delighted too.

Staraku introduced them all to Agumus, and they all thanked him in their own languages.

Agumus held up his hand and silence fell over the group. He spoke with authority, loud enough for everyone to hear. "With forgiveness comes the possibility of friendship!" Staraku repeated him in both the fish and bird languages. Heads nodded gravely as everyone let the wisdom of that lesson sink in.

"Now," Agumus said with a stern look on his face, "let the party begin!"

JOY IS THE SAME IN EVERY LANGUAGE.

And that started the longest and loudest and happiest party that had ever happened on that little island. Birds, fish, trees, Agumus, and Birdfish alike, everyone celebrated. There was no need for translation—joy is the same in every language.

* * *

In the wake of the fire, the island took time to recover. A thick layer of ash coated the leaves, sand, and nests for a time. Coughing could be heard for days as the smoky smell clung to everything and everyone. Waters needed to be cleared.

Despite the needed cleanup, something on island had shifted—something deeper than the depth of the water and higher than the treetops. The birds and the fish saw each other differently. They saw each other as friends.

Among the ones who wanted to work together, apologies became forgiveness. Forgiveness became trust. Old grudges were buried. New friendships were forged. There was a new and wonderful experience spreading through the community. Slowly but surely, the birds and the fish began rebuilding the island. It was truly a fresh start. Rather than rebuilding it exactly as it had been, they rebuilt it in the same way they saved it—together.

They appointed Staraku to a special position on the island. She taught the birds and the fish each other's languages. She planned to tell them all about the trees

and their language eventually, but it was still too soon for any of them to believe her. She laid out plans so they could help each other strengthen the island before the next set of storms came.

Days later, while everyone was working on the island, Staraku felt a tap on her shoulder. To her surprise, she turned to see Tori and Buntu—together.

Tori spoke up first. "Staraku, you've really changed things around here. In a good way. And I just wanted to say sorry for the way I treated you before. To be honest, I was always a little jealous because you were the only bird who could swim too. I felt humiliated that day at The Rock, but I never thanked you for saving me. I just wanted to say I'm sorry. For everything."

Buntu nodded. "Me too. I just didn't want the other fish to make fun of me, so I made life a whole lot harder for you. That wasn't right. I'm sorry too. Thank you for helping us even though we didn't deserve it."

Staraku was shocked. Tori and Buntu were both leaders! *How could they feel afraid too?* But it suddenly made sense as Staraku remembered how many crystals were on the island. *Yes, they felt what I felt.* A small droplet of water fell down Staraku's beak. "Your apologies are accepted."

Staraku thought that was going to be the end of the conversation, but as she turned to leave, Tori asked, "Can you tell us about where you went when you left? And how you got that thing around your neck?"

"My crystal?" Staraku held it up and they shook their heads yes.

They used to be afraid of difference, but now they longed to know what made Staraku different. Yes, she was a Birdfish, but there was also something deeper that set her apart. Something they didn't quite understand. The way she glowed, the way she forgave, her fearlessness. When they saw this, something lit up inside them. Their own sparks of light.

> THEY USED TO BE AFRAID OF DIFFERENCE, BUT NOW THEY LONGED TO KNOW WHAT MADE STARAKU DIFFERENT. YES, SHE WAS A BIRDFISH, BUT THERE WAS ALSO SOMETHING DEEPER THAT SET HER APART...WHEN THEY SAW THIS, SOMETHING LIT UP INSIDE THEM. THEIR OWN SPARKS OF LIGHT.

She told them what her adventure on Crystal Island had taught her. First, she learned how to be safe, anywhere she went. Second, she learned how to apologize and forgive—how to have a pure heart. Third, she learned to respect others—especially for their differences. And on the island, she learned how to bring people together and create harmony in the most unlikely place.

They asked her countless questions.

"You mean this little thing makes it so no one can hurt you?"

"Tell us the story about Rutuma again! About how everyone's made different because they have a different purpose!"

Others had gathered to hear, too, and they listened until the stars glittered above them. Finally, Tori and Buntu worked up the courage to ask what they really longed for deep down.

"Staraku, will you take us to Crystal Island?"

Staraku grinned. She didn't tell them the island's secret—they had crystals waiting just for them. Waiting for this day. Waiting to show them their purpose. But she smiled, because she knew.

Staraku needed to tell Agumus. She searched the island for him, but he was nowhere to be found. "Agumus!" she said under her breath. "I need to talk to you!"

He appeared in front of her, floating down from the trees. Before she could say a word, he looked her in the eyes with the same kindness she first saw in him. It was clear he had something to tell her as well.

"My time here is finished," Agumus said. "My life's purpose is to help those who are lost. You're not lost anymore."

She smiled. "No, I'm not. I'm finally home."

He nodded, a tear in his eye.

Still, she protested. "But what if I ever need you?"

He smiled. "Whenever that is true, I will appear."

"But before you leave, you'll never guess what Tori and Buntu asked me today."

"What?" Agumus acted like he didn't already know what she was going to say.

"Tori and Buntu are lost too. They want me to take them to Crystal Island."

"They will be the first of many you will help, Staraku." The little blue creature gave his glasses a push up his nose, and then spread his arms. Staraku leaned in and they gave each other a hug. "Take them," he whispered. "I'll see you soon."

Staraku left abruptly, without saying a proper good-bye. She ran back down to the beach where Tori and Buntu were waiting. Agumus smiled and called out to her, "Goodbye, Staraku."

Agumus slowly floated up into the sky, just high enough so that he could view a most beautiful sight. Tori took flight from the beach, flying low, close to the water. Buntu swam right beneath the surface. Staraku popped down into the water and back up into the sky—both swimming and flying as she led them.

Agumus watched until they disappeared over the horizon—three friends heading off to Crystal Island—a bird, a fish, and a Birdfish.

ACKNOWLEDGEMENTS

While the story of the Birdfish is incredibly personal to me, it would never have reached its full potential without my entire team.

First, I want to thank my son, Michel, and my daughter, Chanelle. Michel, thank you for being the one to name Agumus. I still remember showing you my sketches of him early on. You pointed to the paper so confidently and stated, "That's Agumus!" I figured, yes, it must be! Chanelle, thank you for your endurance with your busy mother and for reviewing and giving me your insight on the first version of the book.

Thank you to the entire Berry Powell Press team, starting with Carmen Berry, my editor and publisher. You grasped my vision for the book, and you are the reason my message made it to the page. I'm so glad Ida Beerhalter introduced us. As an author, you are my Agumus leading me forward. This book would never have been born without you.

I am beyond grateful to Abigail Dengler, Director of Editorial Services. You invested energy, time, and love to bring my story to life and set me up to share it with the world. Marianne Croonquist, Kathleen Taylor, and Gina Walter enhanced the power of the story with their insight and attention to detail. Valeri Barnes, Senior Editor, elevated the manuscript quality with her editing expertise. Carolyn Rafferty, Director of Publishing, carefully guided the book through the details of the publishing process. Becky Rickett of Big Star Production Group artfully designed my website and online home-base. Roy Carlisle gave generously of his time to provide invaluable publishing guidance.

This book would not be the same without Dee DeLoy, a masterful illustrator, who created the images of Staraku, Agumus, and the rest of the characters. Dee, you poured creativity into every detail. You expertly captured the energy and ultimate joy of my message.

Lastly, I want to thank Matthias Wassermeier for being beside me on this journey. Thank you for loving me, the Birdfish. You remind me of my own power and make me feel like I belong no matter where we are. I don't know where I'd be without your love and support.

ABOUT THE AUTHOR

Katsura **Suzuki, MBA, DBA**, was born in Japan as "the tea ceremony master's daughter." Expected to follow in her mother's footsteps and become a master herself, she was trained in the Japanese meditative arts for thirteen years, starting at age five. However, when she was eighteen, Suzuki decided to carve her own path, going on to build an extremely distinguished thirty-year career in finance, based in Switzerland.

Dr. Suzuki started her career with Ernst & Young, ultimately heading the Japan desk in Zurich for over twenty years. She has since supported the Swiss government, Japanese authorities, and large companies in bridging the intercultural business communication gap between Switzerland and Japan.

Recently, she has shifted to investment, focusing on the technology and health sectors through her own business, Katsura Suzuki GmbH. She is a managing director in a California-based private equity company and President of a family office services company in Switzerland. She has been on the board of directors for seven Japanese-owned client companies, and is a well-recognized mentor, accompanying partner firms on their journey to growth.

Dr. Suzuki is introducing a science-based, inclusive mindfulness approach called The Invisible Gift Method. Her unique and timely message empowers adults and children alike to thrive in an increasingly globalized world. *The Birdfish and the Secret of Crystal Island*, written for children ages 8 – 12 and *The Invisible Gift*, written for adults, teach mindfulness and emotional intelligence principles drawn from the Japanese tea ceremony: tranquility, purity, respect, and harmony.

Dr. Suzuki received her BA in English Literature from Tokyo's Toyo Eiwa Women's College, her MBA from EU Business School in Switzerland, and her DBA from the University of South Australia in Adelaide.

Learn more about Dr. Suzuki at www.drkatsurasuzuki.com.